Noelle

Book Three

Christmas on Dewberry Lane

Cheryl Wright

Noelle

Christmas on Dewberry Lane
Book Three

Copyright ©2020 by Cheryl Wright

Cover Artist: Black Widow Books

Dedication

To Margaret Tanner, my very dear friend and fellow author, for her enduring encouragement and friendship.

To Alan, my husband of over forty-six years, who has been a relentless supporter of my writing and dreams for many years.

To Virginia McKevitt, cover artist and friend, who always creates the most amazing covers for my books.

To You, my wonderful readers, who encourage me to continue writing these stories. It is such a joy knowing so many of you enjoy reading my stories as much as I love writing them for you.

Table of Contents

Chapter One

Dewberry Lane, Dewberry, Montana

November 1880

Noelle Jenkins flipped the closed sign on the door of her little store, *Book Time*. It was book club night, and she needed to prepare for her small group of ladies who would be arriving soon.

She had the kettle filled and on the wood stove, the mugs were ready, and the light refreshments she'd bought were prepared for serving. It was a little extra work added to her day, but these ladies came each and every week. That meant she had guaranteed sales for the *Book of the Week.*

This week's book was a little different than most, but it was the one her customers chose. *Heart Flutterings by* H.C. Clifford-Jones was definitely not Noelle's first choice, but her ladies had demanded something a little more lighthearted this time around and that's what they got.

"Good evening, ladies," Noelle said as they began to stream through the door. Each woman clung to her copy of *Heart Flutterings* as though their lives depended on it. It was somewhat amusing, but Noelle was very aware many of her book club ladies were more than a little lonely. *Book Time* was their happy place, and they all felt very safe here.

The chairs were placed in a circle to ensure no one was left out, and everyone took a seat. They clutched their well-worn copy of the book and waited for Noelle to begin. She took a deep breath and let it out slowly. "Did everyone finish reading the book?" She glanced about, pleased they had all completed it. "Shall we begin then? Who would like to go first?"

Three hands shot up, and Noelle chose the newcomer to their group, Mrs. Halliday. "It was wonderful," she almost swooned. "I particularly liked the part where he asked to court her." The woman was beaming, and several of the other women rolled their eyes.

"That's lovely," Noelle said. "Mrs. Carson, what did you think?"

"The book was fairly well written, and I do like a bit of romance," she said, color blooming in her cheeks, "but this was a bit soppy for me. I'd rather something I can get my teeth into. Like a mystery."

"Oh, but I loved it," Mrs. Herbert said, not waiting to be asked.

Suddenly, everyone stopped talking and Noelle turned to follow the direction of their gazes. A tall man with dark tousled hair filled the doorway and stared out over them. Hadn't she locked the main door? She normally did and would have sworn she did so tonight.

She stood and turned to him. "May I help you?" She stared into his face and thought he seemed vaguely familiar.

His expression was one of amusement. He suddenly reached out his hand. "H…er, Howie Jones."

Did the man not know his own name? It made Noelle more than a little suspicious. "What can I do for you Mr. Jones? As you can see, we're in the middle of something here." She knew it was rude to do so, but Noelle continued to stare. There was something about the man. "I am Noelle Jenkins. I own this bookstore."

He strolled uninvited toward the extra chairs at the side of the store and grabbed one, insinuating himself into the book club circle. Everyone moved their chairs back a little to allow him access. "Do you mind?" His gaze moved around the circle, and no one dared say no.

"I'm afraid you can't stay, Mr. Jones. We are discussing our Book of the Week and you won't be familiar with it."

He chuckled then rubbed his hand across his chin. "I am very familiar with it," he said, gazing down at the book languishing on Mrs. Herbert's lap.

Mrs. Grayson was studying the man, her gaze never leaving him.

Suddenly, mutterings began around the room. Noelle wasn't sure if her ladies were upset there was a man in their midst, or if it was something else entirely. "I think you should leave, Mr. Jones. As you can see, your presence has upset the ladies."

"Does anyone want me to go?" He addressed those present and appeared prepared to leave. "I refuse to stay against anyone's wishes."

Noelle's heart thudded. She didn't know this stranger, and apparently neither did anyone else. She worried what would happen if she demanded he leave. Would he become violent or abusive? She admonished herself for not locking the door. It was a habit she had, and it had never let her down, until now.

"I know who you are," Mrs. Grayson suddenly accused.

Noelle heard the collective gasp and waited impatiently for all to be revealed. Instead of conceding, he put a finger to his lips and the older lady grinned, a glint to her eye.

"Shall we continue," he asked, and so they did.

"I'm very pleased I heard about this book club meeting," he said when the discussion ended. "It is always fascinating to hear what others enjoy or detest about m...a book." He'd been an active participant in the discussions, which made Noelle even more curious about *Mr. Jones*. She still wasn't convinced that was his real name, but was intrigued about the mysterious visitor.

Mrs. Grayson pierced him with a scowl. "Now that the proceedings are over, I do think you should be truthful, *Mr. Jones*." Her lips were pulled into a straight line, and it was obvious the woman was somewhat displeased with their guest. "Or should I reveal your true identity?"

Gasps could be heard all around the circle.

He stood and bowed to everyone in the room. "Thank you for allowing me to stay, ladies. I do appreciate it."

"Oh, for goodness sakes," Mrs. Grayson said, more than a little impatient now. "This is H.C. Clifford-Jones, author of the book we've just been discussing. Am I wrong, Mr. Jones?"

He turned to her and grinned. "No, Madam, you are correct. Forgive my deception, ladies, but I prefer to hear feedback from the horse's mouth, so to speak."

There was outrage, and several of the ladies glared at Noelle. "Miss Jenkins was totally unaware of my visit or my identity." He was quick to defend her, which pleased Noelle. After all, she needed the group to have faith in her for future book club meetings.

"Shall we have supper now?" She hurried into the small kitchen without waiting for a response. She felt his presence behind her and was most unhappy. "Can I help you, *Mr. Jones*?" She emphasized his fake name, for his benefit, and to show how displeased she was with his trickery.

"Actually, Jones is my real name. My publisher felt it was far too ordinary so took my middle name of Clifford and hyphenated the two names." He raised his eyebrows and stared at her.

It did not appease Noelle at all. "It was still deception," she said under her breath then struggled past him with a tray filled with coffees and cake.

"Let me." He took the tray from her, and despite her anger at the man, Noelle was grateful for the reprieve. She grappled with the tray every week due to the sheer weight of it. It was the least he could do to make up for his duplicity, not only to her, but the entire book club group.

"Supper, ladies," he announced as he entered the room. The scoundrel made it sound as though he was the one who'd supplied and prepared the refreshments. Inwardly, Noelle was fuming. Outwardly, she maintained her composure, ensuring she was the perfect hostess.

As everyone sat with their coffee and cake, silence overtook them. The quiet was shattered by a male voice. "What are we reading next?"

All eyes turned to him. Mrs. Grayson looked somewhat amused at his question, while Mrs. Jensen looked totally stunned. The man had insinuated himself into their little book club, and now wanted a repeat performance? How utterly rude of him.

"I don't think—" Noelle didn't a chance to finish her sentence.

"—Oh. And here I was thinking Mr. Jones fit in so well." It was typical of Mrs. Grayson. She loved to stir people up, and she was doing an exceptional job of that tonight.

"I…well…"

"It's all right, Miss Jenkins." He threw back the last of his coffee and began to stand. "Thank you, ladies, for having me." Howie Jones headed toward the entrance to the store and Noelle followed.

"Don't leave, Mr. Jones." Mrs. Grayson's voice cut through the silence, and Noelle was ready to throttle the old dear. The man was almost at the door, and she was ready to see the back of him. "It was quite fun having you here tonight. Wasn't it, ladies?" She glanced around the room and not a soul disagreed.

Noelle sighed. She found the author rather overbearing. Not that he'd taken over the meeting. She'd been grateful for him sitting back and listening most of the time. It was after all, his book, and it would be uncouth to praise his own story. At least that was her opinion.

"Tell me, Mrs. Grayson," he said, turning to face the older woman. "What book are you reading next week?" There was a twinkle to his eye and a slight lift to his lips. The dastardly man was enjoying himself. He was intolerable.

"Perhaps you would help us choose. What do we think, ladies? Should we invite Mr. Jones back next week?"

The exuberance in the room to have him return was outrageous. Noelle did not want the man to return. It was bad enough he turned up unannounced, but to be invited by her book club ladies was shameful. She'd not even been given a choice!

"I would be honored." He turned to Noelle. "That is, provided our lovely hostess agrees." He pierced her with his gaze, daring her to refuse.

"That would be delightful." It really wouldn't be, but who was she to disagree with her paying customers?

He strolled toward the shelves lining the little store and began to peruse some titles. "What do you normally read? I'm sure your choice in books goes far beyond my frivolous story of this week. A little mystery perhaps? A saga? Oh, wait. A grizzly murder or two." He glanced around the room to see most of the group pulling faces at the last suggestion.

"What about this one?" Mrs. Carson pulled a fairly new addition from the shelf. "*Kathleen's Burden*. It sounds rather interesting, don't you think?"

Noelle thought hard. She was almost certain she had enough copies to go around. "An excellent choice, Mrs. Carson. What does everyone think?"

There was mutual agreement, and she checked the storeroom. There were enough copies to go around plus a number of extras, which was excellent. There were times the ladies had to share a copy since there weren't enough. *Kathleen's Burden* was already a bestseller, so she'd taken a chance. Besides, recommendations were generally accepted by her group of ladies.

"Thank you, Mrs. Grayson," Noelle said as she placed the book in a brown carry bag. She noticed the woman's driver waiting out front so knew her customer would get home safe. The other women had all been collected by their husbands, which left only herself and Mr. Jones to leave.

He carried the supper tray out to the tiny kitchen, which Noelle knew she should appreciate but wished he would just go home. Which made her ponder, where was his home? He didn't live around Dewberry, she was certain. Perhaps he was staying at the hotel on the outskirts of town. It wasn't her problem, so she wouldn't ask.

He continued to linger while she tidied up; even helped move the chairs back where they belonged. She had to admit, the man was helpful when she was certain he wouldn't be.

"Well," she said, putting on her coat and gloves and picking up her bag. "It is time to say goodnight." She locked the door when they were both outside and turned to walk home. Mr. Jones followed. Noelle turned to face him. "Are you following me, Mr. Jones?" She was becoming quite annoyed with the man now.

"You could say that, Miss Jenkins. I am merely doing what any gentleman should – I am seeing you home safely." Her back stiffened. Was he mad? Did he honestly think she would let a total stranger accompany her home? "Besides, we are going in the same direction. I'm staying at the Dewberry Hotel."

"Oh. My house is about two blocks past there." Perhaps she was wrong about him. After all, he'd been quite useful when she was tidying up. Not to mention carrying the supper tray for her. And the ladies did seem to like him. "How long are you staying in Dewberry?" She was curious since he'd practically forced himself on the group for next week. He'd also purchased a copy of the book; the same as the other book club members.

"I'm not certain at this point," he said, bringing himself to stand next to her. He put his arm out for her to take and Noelle reluctantly accepted. It wasn't as though she'd not walked home alone before, because she did it every week. Admittedly, it did get rather intimidating at times. Especially once she was out of Dewberry Lane. It was so open once she was out of town, and Noelle always hurried when she was past that boundary.

She studied him as he glanced about. "You do this every week after book club?" He stared at her until she answered with a nod. "It's not safe for you to be out alone. Even your older ladies are collected by their husbands."

Noelle was about to disagree when she realized what he said was true. There was very little crime in Dewberry, and it was rarely violence against individuals when it did occur. Petty theft and teenage stunts were more the problem, but it did happen. She'd been lucky, and Noelle knew it.

"It's only once a week, Mr. Jones."

He stared down at her, a scowl on his face. "It only takes one time for you to find yourself in danger. And please, call me Howie."

"Then you must call me Noelle." She couldn't very well force him to address her formally when he insisted on her being casual, could she? "Here we are at your hotel. Thank you for walking with me, and goodnight, Mr. er, Howie."

He stared at her, a stunned look on his face. "I think you are mistaken, Noelle," he said, as he continued to walk with her. "I said I'd see you home safely, and that's exactly what I shall do."

She felt more comfortable walking home with an escort, there was no doubt. But in the matter of a few hours, H.C. Clifford-Jones, aka Howie Jones, had insinuated himself into her life.

Noelle wasn't sure how she felt about that.

Chapter Two

"I enjoyed book club last night. Mr. Jones was rather pleasant." Mrs. Grayson gave her a penetrating look, daring Noelle to disagree. She refused to do that, knowing the woman would start a discussion of sorts. It would end up lasting far too long and wasting Noelle's precious time.

Mrs. Grayson was by far her best customer. Undeniably, she was the best customer of practically every store on Dewberry Lane. If she wasn't buying for herself, she would be helping someone in need. At least she didn't squander her riches and flaunt her wealth to all and sundry. She did a lot of good with what she had available. That was even more evident at Christmas.

Glancing up from wrapping the woman's purchases, Noelle smiled. "Yes, he is. Did you know Howie walked me home last night?"

She raised her eyebrows at Noelle. "It's Howie now, is it?" She never missed a trick and would use it to her benefit.

"He's a nice young man, is that Mr. Jones." Mrs. Grayson nodded as if agreeing with herself.

Noelle passed the package over, and added the purchases to Mrs. Grayson's account. "He's staying at the Dewberry Hotel, so it wasn't far out of his way."

"I know."

The cunning old dear probably set it all up if truth be told. After playing matchmaker with Holly Yates and Marcus Taylor, Noelle would put nothing past her.

She glanced across as the door opened. Her heart did a little dance when she saw him standing in the doorway. "Good morning."

Mrs. Grayson stared at her, a smirk on her face. Did she set them up – yet again? Had she asked the handsome man to call in today?

"Good morning, Mr. Jones," she said, still grinning. "We were just discussing you – your ears must be burning." She had no shame, that was for sure. The last thing Noelle wanted was for the smug Howie Jones to believe he was a point of discussion.

"Indeed?"

"I appreciate you walking Miss Jenkins home last night. I tell her every week it's not safe."

His gaze pierced Noelle. "I told her the same thing. At least we both know she got home safely last night. The same will occur next week as well."

"Thank you, Mr. Jones. I knew I could count on you."

So she was right – Mrs. Grayson had set it up with him. The fact he was going in the same direction was irrelevant. All the same, she did appreciate the company and not having to worry about being accosted along the way.

"Yes, thank you, Howie. I do appreciate it. Is there something I can do for you?"

"Most certainly. You can accompany me to lunch." He turned to Mrs. Grayson. "Do you have any suggestions?"

"*Ma's Kitchen* would do nicely. It's the only diner for miles around, and the food is good."

Noelle was fuming. They were making decisions about where she would eat without bothering to check if she even accepted his invitation. "Don't mind me," she said off-handedly, then stormed out to the kitchen. She heard quiet mutterings, and then a door slammed shut. Hopefully, it was Howie Jones leaving, and it would be the last she would see of him.

How utterly rude, making decisions on her behalf without bothering to consult her. "Miss Jenkins. Noelle." He stuck his head around the corner of the kitchen. "I apologize. I shouldn't have assumed but waited for your answer."

At least he had the decency to apologize. Most men wouldn't bother and would try to force her to go anyway. Howie stepped into the kitchen and it suddenly seemed far smaller than a few moments ago. He was a tall man, solid too. It was more of a kitchenette than a kitchen, and he almost filled the space, leaving little room for her.

Noelle glanced up into his face. How could she refuse after an apology like that? He sounded sincere too, which made it even more difficult.

His chocolate brown eyes stared down at her and she saw the sincerity there. A clump of his mousy brown hair fell forward as he leaned toward her, and Noelle wanted nothing more but to brush it back for him. The thought caused her to pause. She'd met this man less than twenty-four hours ago, and she was already having such thoughts? It was far from acceptable.

Darn him, and darn Mrs. Grayson too. The woman was a menace to society.

"Thank you for the offer, Howie. I'll be with you in a few moments. Take a seat in the store if you will?"

His eyes opened wide in surprise. Did he think she would refuse him? Did Mrs. Grayson tell him she would be hard to convince? Noelle just bet she did. Well, she would show both of them. She checked herself in the mirror, fixing her hair, then strolled out into the store as though nothing was amiss.

And what's more, Noelle would ensure she enjoyed her meal with Howie Jones if it were the last thing she did.

"The meal was lovely, thank you." Noelle wiped her lips with the linen napkin and glanced across at him. Surprisingly, Howie Jones was good company. They'd chatted about his books and about her bookstore.

It seemed neither of them had much of a life outside their occupations. Howie wanted to change that – for both of them. Not that there was much to do around Dewberry, but she'd offered to show him around. They agreed to a picnic lunch at the park tomorrow, weather allowing. He would pick her up at noon, and they would take a stroll. It would give him an opportunity to see the various stores along the way, and they'd have a chance to talk. To get to know each other before the next book club meeting.

Howie helped her into her coat, and they headed back to *Book Time*. A new shipment was due this afternoon, and Noelle would be kept busy checking it and placing the books on the shelves. Howie offered to help. "Are you not working on a new book?" Perhaps he was here on holiday. But that seemed unlikely. Dewberry wasn't a tourist destination since it was so far from anything. The nearest town was over a hundred miles away.

"I am," he said as they stepped out into the cold air. Flurries swirled down from the sky and landed on their hair. He reached out and brushed them away for her. She glanced up into his face then quickly pulled her gaze away. The man was mesmerizing, and it was the last thing she wanted.

"What are you writing? Or am I not supposed to ask such questions?" She smiled and he grinned.

"It's not a secret. My publisher is already promoting it." He rolled his eyes, and Noelle laughed.

"Isn't that a bit premature?"

He offered her his arm. "Very much so, but they want to drum up sales before the book releases. The truth is," he turned to face her, "I had far too many distractions at home and needed somewhere quiet to write. Someone suggested Dewberry, and here I am."

"I see."

"Do you?"

She contemplated him. "I guess that means you are here until the book is finished, however long that might be."

"That is correct. It can take anything from a few weeks to a few months to finish a book." He stared down at his damp shoes, and she wondered what he was thinking. Or was it his way of saying *Don't get used to me, I'll soon be gone*? Either way, Noelle needed to remember he was only here temporarily, no matter what else happened. Her heart hammered in her chest. For some reason, she felt sad to think he wouldn't be around for long, which was crazy. Between Howie and Mrs. Grayson, she felt annoyed they'd conspired together for Howie to win her affections.

Despite it being confirmed he would leave when his work was done, she wanted to get to know him better. It wasn't going to happen though. Noelle couldn't let herself become attracted to this man when he'd made it clear he *would* leave in a few months time. From this moment on, she would treat him like a friend and ensure she didn't get too close. "Here we are." She pulled the key out of her pocket and went to open the door. Howie's glove-clad hand covered hers, and a thrill ran through her.

"Let me."

She glanced up at him. His brown eyes seemed so sad. Was he feeling the same way she did? That he needed to keep his distance? They had chemistry, there was no doubting it, but if nothing could ever come of it, they needed to stay friends and nothing more.

Why did it feel as though her heart had shattered into a million pieces?

Noelle flipped the sign on the door to *closed* then locked the door. As she wandered back into the store to tidy up, she heard a tapping sound. The last thing she needed was a late customer. If she stayed much longer, she'd be walking home in the darkness, which she detested.

She turned back to find Howie standing there, a huge smile on his face. She'd missed him this afternoon, which was crazy. Two days ago, she didn't even know the man. Today, she was pining for him. She took a deep breath and let it out slowly. She'd vowed to keep her distance, and that was what she intended to do.

Friends only. She repeated the mantra over and over. Noelle must keep it in mind – he would be gone before she knew it.

She opened the door and he came inside without an invitation, which was annoying. It was snowing, so she'd give him that; it was cold out there.

He brushed the snow from his coat then slowly straightened up. She watched his every move before checking herself and forcing her gaze away. "It's cold out there." He lifted a hand and began moving it toward her then stopped himself. Was he thinking along the same lines as she was?

"What are you doing here?" She didn't mean to sound so abrupt, but she couldn't help what was done.

He studied her then pulled off his coat. "I thought it was obvious. I've come to walk you home. It's already getting dark."

Oh. And she'd been rude to him about being here. She really needed to stop being disappointed in the situation and letting her feelings get away with her. Noelle had never been a person who allowed her emotions to show through, but for some reason, Howie got under her skin. Was it because Mrs. Grayson had made it happen?

What was she now anyway, the Dewberry Matchmaker? It certainly seemed that way, but she should be grateful. If for no other reason but to have

Howie get her home safe and sound each night. Except that it wouldn't last. Once he was gone from Dewberry, she'd be right back where she started. Alone and afraid.

"I have to finish tidying up before I can leave." She could leave it until the morning, but she preferred to have a fresh start each day.

"I can help," he said, then began straightening the chairs as well as the uneven books on the shelf. It was a good feeling knowing he appreciated books in the same way she did. Soon, they were done, and he helped her into her coat. He put on his own coat and they left the store.

It was snowing quite heavily by the time they got outside again, and Noelle wrapped a scarf around her neck. "It's not looking good for our picnic tomorrow." She glanced up at him and Howie looked disappointed.

"Guess we'll see. At least I know I can get you home safely." Moonlight peaked through as the snow drifted downward and gave them some light to find their way home.

"I know I haven't said it before, but I do appreciate your company on the walk home." It made her feel all warm and fuzzy to tell him so, but it probably meant nothing to him.

"I enjoy your company too, so it's rather selfish on my part." He stared at her as though daring her to disagree. She nodded but said not a word. Besides, he made her feel more than a little protected. She hadn't felt comfortable walking home unaccompanied for an awfully long time. Ever since a gang of youths had attacked old Mr. Harbison on the other side of town and left him for dead.

The thought of the old man lying there, bleeding in the cold and the dark, sent shivers down her spine. It was over a year ago now, and the youths were caught and punished, but that didn't alter the fact it had left her shattered. Afraid of her own shadow as she made her way home.

"What are you thinking about? The color has drained from your face."

Should she tell him? Would he even care? Noelle knew the answer was that he would care, and by his own admission, he cared about her. She stopped walking and turned to face him. "An old man was attacked one night and nearly died. It's scary out here now."

He pulled her closer. "You're shaking, and I suspect it's not from the cold." She glanced up at him, a huge lump in her throat. She leaned her head against his chest, all the time knowing she shouldn't.

"Mr. Harbison had been in the bookstore a few times, but apart from that, I didn't really know him."

Howie tightened his grip on her and ran a hand across her back. "I won't let anything happen to you," he said gently.

For now. After he left Dewberry, everything would go back to the way it was before, and they both knew it. They stood quietly for a few minutes then continued their walk to Noelle's cottage, neither of them saying another word.

Chapter Three

Howie saw Noelle into her house and waited for her to lock the door behind her.

She was still upset, he could tell, but he reluctantly walked away. He worried about her, more than he should, given he'd only known her a short time. What would she do once he left Dewberry? No woman should be left to walk home alone, and most especially in the darkness. The snow made it a double-edged sword. The visibility was even worse when it was snowing.

He was already growing rather fond of this quiet little town, not to mention the bookstore owner. Dewberry was set in the middle of nowhere, and there were few people here compared to Helena, where he lived. But so far, it hadn't bothered him. When he'd arrived, the last thing on his mind was meeting someone he would feel any sort of affection for. Heck, he didn't even know the place existed until his publisher told him the tiny bookstore had ordered a number of his books. It had piqued his interest and Howie needed to find out more. When he discovered the book club would be discussing his book, he'd made his way here.

Twisting the truth a little about his intentions for being here was a bit far fetched, but he *was* writing. Just not as much as he'd made out.

He reached his hotel and the aroma of freshly cooked food hit his senses as he walked past the dining area. He couldn't resist, and Howie made his way into the small dining room. After being seated and making his order, a thought hit him – how much better would it be with Noelle sitting opposite him right now? He tried to shrug the notion away, but it wouldn't go. It was then he knew he was smitten.

It was the last thing he needed right now – a woman to distract him from his work but it seemed it was already too late. How did that old saying go? *The heart wants what the heart wants.*

They had chemistry. Howie had known it from almost the moment they'd met. The question was, did Noelle realize it too? The delicious smell of a thick steak under his nose pulled his thoughts away from questions of the heart and turned them to matters of the stomach. ~*~

The day had barely begun, but already Noelle felt disappointed. Snow was falling heavily and the picnic would have to be cancelled. That meant she wouldn't get to see Howie today. Her brows joined together as she thought about that some more. Why should she even care the picnic was off? Howie was a new acquaintance, not someone she'd known for a long time. The front door opened, letting in the cold. A small amount of snow blew through to where she stood behind the counter. *It sure was chilly.*

She glanced across at the fireplace. The logs were still burning, but getting a little low. She would attend to that as soon as this customer was gone. Noelle closed the account book she'd been working on and immediately felt eyes on her. She knew it was him before she'd even looked up.

"Good morning, Noelle," he said as he approached the front counter. "It's a pity about the weather." His expression said it all. He was every bit as disappointed as she was.

"It really is. Perhaps next time. Is there something I can do for you, or did you come here to tell me about the weather?" She smiled, hoping he would take it in the manner it was meant.

"I've come to ask a favor, if I may?" It was then she noticed the notebook under his arm. "It is far too noisy at the hotel, and I wondered if you'd mind…"

She knew what he was about to say before it was out of his mouth. "Let you work here? Of course. Pull a chair to the fireplace and do whatever it is you do."

He breathed a sigh of relief. "Thank you."

"I won't disturb you?" He'd already pulled the chair near the fireplace and was eyeing off the logs sitting nearby. She went closer and kneeled at almost the same time he did.

He reached for a piece of cut wood – at the same time she did – and their hands touched. A shiver ran down her spine. He glanced across at her, which had Noelle thinking he'd felt it too. "I…I'm sorry," she said, her confidence all but gone. "I can do this. You have work to do."

"So do you," he said quietly. "I didn't come here to interrupt you, but that's exactly what I've done."

He threw a log on the low burning fire, and pushed it around with the fire-poker. Noelle was mesmerized by the glowing embers. She'd never felt this way before, and it bothered her. She'd only ever been interested in her work at the bookstore, and now this…infatuation…was affecting her concentration. She had books to catalog and put away on the shelves. She also needed to sort out the storeroom and add her excess books there.

Hopefully, her book club ladies would be interested in her suggestion for their next book. That in turn, would help with her storage space.

"I was about to make coffee. Would you like one? It will warm you up."

His smile went all the way to his eyes. Noelle liked it when he smiled – it lit up his face and made him even more handsome than he was when he didn't smile. "That would be lovely," he said. "Thanks." He put his notebook aside and followed her into the kitchen. The heat from the fire didn't extend this far, and it was quite chilly in there at times. That was definitely the case today.

She filled the mugs and felt his warmth behind her. Noelle knew she could get used to having him around. It often got lonely at the store, especially if there were few customers on a given day. What if she got used to him coming in to write on a daily basis and suddenly, he was gone? How would she feel then? Her heart thudded. She wasn't sure she would cope with the sudden loss, even after a week or two. After all, that could be all it takes, especially if he had the quiet he required.

Hands shaking, she handed over his coffee and they sat at the small table that was pushed aside to make the kitchen roomier. He studied her, and Noelle knew he'd picked up on her mood.

Despite her misgivings, she denied it. "Everything is fine," she lied, then reached for a tin of biscuits. "Sorry, I don't have any cake today. That's reserved for book club night."

"It was nice cake indeed. Did you make it?" He sipped his coffee and studied her over the rim of his mug.

"Goodness no. I buy it from the *Holly-Berry Cake Shoppe*. It's just a few doors down."

He studied her for a little longer before speaking again. "Good. I've ordered our picnic from there."

She almost spat out her coffee. "In case you hadn't noticed, it's snowing. You know that white stuff that almost covered your coat when you were outside." Noelle couldn't help but grin.

He pretended to be pained by her words. "Were sitting in your kitchen now. Yes, it's tiny, but big enough for us to sit and eat." Now he smiled. "We're having an indoor picnic."

Warmth flooded her. The man was so considerate. "That sounds really nice," she said. "I'm looking forward to it."

He stood and took his mug to the sink. "Leave it. I'll tidy up – you get back to your writing." He nodded and left her alone. Two days ago, Noelle didn't even know Howie Jones. Now, she couldn't imagine her life without him.

At ten minutes to noon, Howie packed his notebook away and Noelle stored it under the counter where it couldn't be damaged or stolen. He then headed to the *Holly-Berry Cake Shoppe*. He'd left no specific instructions, only asked for a good assortment of food for a picnic for two. The look on the woman's face was priceless. She looked relieved when he explained they'd be eating indoors.

It turned out Holly was a friend of Noelle's, so she knew exactly what to include. There were chicken pies as well as egg and bacon pies. She'd also included some cupcakes and slices. Combined with coffee, they would have a lovely lunch at the bookstore. Howie was truly looking forward to it.

Despite the cold and the snow, Howie strolled back to the bookstore with a skip in his step. He even found himself whistling at one point but forced himself to abruptly stop. What would people think?

He shook himself. Since when did H.C. Clifford-Jones care what people thought? Or Howie Jones for that matter. Until now, he'd only cared about himself. Meeting Noelle Jenkins changed all that. The demure woman had gotten under his skin and into his heart. Now he was second-guessing himself. When he'd first set foot in Dewberry, he'd almost got right back on that stagecoach and went home again. What everyone had described as a quaint little town, he'd seen as an isolated place that was almost akin to a ghost town. When he wasn't writing, he liked to be around people. Dewberry had few of those.

Well, if you compared it to Helena, anyway.

He stood outside *Book Time* and noticed Noelle huddled around the fire. An idea came to him, but he wasn't sure it would come to fruition. Instead of pondering it further, standing out in the snow and the freezing weather, he went inside where it was far warmer.

"Lunch is here," he called, hoping there were no customers. He certainly hadn't seen any from outside.

Noelle straightened and turned to him. "Good. I'm starving." She scurried over to the door and locked it then put up the closed sign.

Everything had been carefully packed into a wicker basket, supplied by Noelle's friend Holly. Inside the basket he found a little note. "Enjoy" it said, and he wondered if she did that for all her customers. Howie seriously doubted it. As if it wasn't enough having Mrs. Grayson as a matchmaker, it looked like Holly was trying her best to match them up as well. It made perfect sense now – she'd smirked almost the entire time he was there.

He carried the basket into the kitchenette, but it was quite cold in there. "It's a pity we can't sit near the fire," he said. The last thing Noelle needed was for food to be spilled and spoil her books.

"Stop what you're doing," she said urgently, and he froze. What could be so important? He glanced up at her and waited for further instructions.

She reached into one of the drawers and pulled out a large tablecloth. "Who says we can't sit by the fire?" Noelle grinned at him, and he felt bolts of lightning run through his veins at the thought of their close proximity. He followed her out to the main room and waited while she spread the tablecloth. It had been years since Howie had been on a picnic, and as far as he could recall, he'd never had one inside.

He felt her eyes on him as he unloaded the basket. "Your friend Holly seems to have given us far more than I expected. I doubt we'll be able to eat all this."

"She's an amazing cook. It won't go to waste, even if we don't eat it all now."

"These pies are still warm," he said, his mouth salivating at the thought. He placed them on the plates Noelle had provided, and they said a blessing before they began to eat. It was nice sitting here by the fire, but even better given the company he had. Slowly, his bones that had felt like blocks of ice, began to thaw. Warmth began to flood him and he felt near normal again. "This was a great idea," he said as he took a bite of the chicken pie. The taste tickled his taste buds, and he couldn't remember ever eating such a tasty pie. It was good country food like his mother used to make. "Delicious too."

She took a dainty bite of an egg and bacon pie and he savored the moment. They would never have this particular memory again. It was one he was sure he'd remember forever. It may not seem special to others, but to Howie, it was a highlight in his life.

"It's really good. I don't know how she does it. I wish I could cook as good as she does." He studied her. She wasn't jealous like he'd known some women to be. Noelle was praising her friend. She was a good person, and that was evident that first night. She was more interested in protecting her book club ladies than worrying about herself.

Upon finishing the chicken pie, he reached out for an egg and bacon pie. It was still warm as well. Noelle handed him a napkin, and their hands touched. Shivers went down his spine. He stared into her eyes. Noelle's were open wide. Without a doubt, she had felt it too. They were strangers, the pair of them. Strangers who, without their consent, had found themselves in a unique situation. One where they had no say in the matter.

The Lord had chosen them to be together, and now it was up to them to make it work.

Days had passed since Howie began to write in the bookstore. He had the odd interruption when a customer recognized him and he was forced to chat with them, but he didn't seem to mind. Noelle found it comforting having him there, and apart from when he took a break, she mostly wouldn't have known he was in the store.

She went about her business, and he went about his writing. When a delivery came in, he stopped work and helped her with the boxes. She hadn't asked, but he insisted. Since *Book Time* was the only bookstore for a hundred miles, she was blessed with a steady stream of sales. The book club certainly helped with that. Word had spread that H.C. Clifford-Jones would be at the next one, resulting in additional bookings. Noelle would need to keep track, otherwise, she wouldn't be able to fit them all in the limited space she had. On the plus side, those ladies had each bought a copy of the book they would be discussing.

"It's bizarre that I suddenly have new ladies wanting to join book club." She hadn't meant to be so blatant, but it did amuse her somewhat.

"Funny that," Howie said as he sipped his coffee. "They do realize I won't be around forever?"

She nodded and went back to her coffee. But the reinforcement that he would be gone, possibly in a matter of weeks, left her feeling empty.

It had become a habit to close up the store for fifteen minutes every day at ten. They would sit by the fire with their hot beverages and chat. Howie needed a break from writing and Noelle...well she enjoyed his company. How she would cope once he was gone, she wasn't certain. She would continue on with her life, thinking about him daily, no doubt. It had been made harder by the fact he was here every day, in close proximity.

Howie, on the other hand, would likely go back to the life he had before and not think about her ever again.

"Shall we dine together tonight?" His voice came out of the blue, and it startled her. Noelle stared at him over the rim of her mug.

"I have the Christmas Extravaganza meeting tonight. I'm sorry." And she was. Most of the time those meetings were a waste of time, and honestly, she wasn't certain they did anything for the individual stores.

"Then we shall work around it. You go to your meeting, and we'll eat together afterwards."

It sounded good, and it also meant she wouldn't be walking home in the dark. "Thank you. I'd like that." She glanced across at the clock. It was time to open the doors again. Such a pity; she was enjoying her alone time with Howie. As she unlocked the door, two customers appeared.

Howie accompanied Noelle to her meeting, which wasn't far down Dewberry Lane, then, at her suggestion, went back to the bookstore to write.

He'd felt somewhat uncomfortable when she'd handed him the keys to her store, but it also made him feel warm and fuzzy. It was an indication she trusted him, despite their short acquaintance. Before settling in for a writing session, he threw a small log on the fire, trying to keep the place warm.

Glancing about, he knew he could get used to this place. Get used to writing here and could most certainly get used to the woman who owned it. In fact, he already had. He stared down at the notebook in his hands, and the title scrawled across the front. *Hannah's Ambition*. This was the sort of book he preferred to write – mystery with a spattering of romantic elements. Although, given the choice, the latter would be gone. His publisher was endeavoring to have his books appeal to the female audience more by including some romance. If the book club was anything to go by, it had certainly worked. But he wouldn't be doing that again. *Heart Flutterings* was pure romance, and although he'd enjoyed writing it, and the ladies obviously enjoyed reading it, he preferred to have at least some mystery in his books.

He'd done well with his mystery books, so Howie had no idea why his publisher wanted to play around with his storylines like this. *Hannah Halstead* was the protagonist in most of his books. No other writer had used a female protagonist, so his books had an appeal no others did. It was the sole reason his books had been contracted. Howie didn't kid himself – he wasn't the best writer around, but he was a good storyteller. Being around people helped him with that; as he listened to the constant chatter in shops and restaurants, it helped him to write his books. Dewberry gave him a different perspective; it let him get closer to people and see another side to them.

He opened his notebook and pulled his chair closer to the fire. He wondered how long Noelle's meeting would last. Trying to force his way into the meeting to ensure her safety hadn't worked, but he hadn't thought for a moment it would. Howie rolled his shoulders and lifted his pencil; it was time to get to work.

The knock at the front door startled him. Howie suddenly jumped up – it had to be Noelle. He approached the door, unlocked it, and pulled her inside. She was covered in snow and her teeth were chattering. Had she been standing out there long?

"Good Lord! You're like an icicle. Stand next to the fire." He locked the door then dragged her to the low burning fire. He hadn't kept it at a roaring level since it would need to be out before they left the store for the night.

"If we're going out, there's not a lot of point," she said, huddling near the fire, regardless. "I have to admit, I'm famished."

He stared at her then grinned. "I admit to being famished myself." He poked about at the fire, pushing logs aside until there were only a few embers left.

They almost ran to *Ma's Kitchen*, where Howie had made a late booking. The food at the hotel was good, but he had no intention of taking Noelle there. The place was full of riffraff and ruffians. It was fine for him, but he wouldn't take a lady like Noelle into such a situation.

Being so late in the evening, their choices were few, but roast lamb was still available. They both ordered that, along with apple pie for dessert. The diner would close in a little over half an hour, which gave them just enough time to eat.

"It's lovely here by the fire," Noelle said quietly. The reflection of the flames flickering across her face fascinated him, and Howie couldn't pull his gaze away. He slid his hand across the table and covered her own. A bold move, and she was likely to drag her hand away, but it was a risk he was willing to take.

"It is a definite contrast to the outside weather." He watched as she smiled, and he squeezed her hand. He shouldn't be doing this – getting so close to her – and they both knew it. They were mere acquaintances on a limited time frame. The moment his book was finished, he would return to Helena. The only way to extend that was to drag out the completion of his book, but even then, he would be taking a risk. On the one hand, *Hannah's Ambition* was going well and almost writing itself. On the other hand, he wasn't really here to write anything.

A cold shiver suddenly went through him. He was being far from honest with Noelle, and that wasn't fair. To either of them.

"Oh, that looks delicious," Noelle said as their meal arrived. "Thank you." She glanced up at Merry Jensen, who owned *Ma's Kitchen*, and smiled. Warmth flooded him. If there was only one thing Howie knew, it was without a doubt, he needed to leave Dewberry before he became even more enchanted by the little bookstore owner.

Chapter Four

"I'm so pleased you were able to come to church today." Noelle smiled up at him and Howie's heart thudded. He hadn't told her he'd be leaving soon. He would stay for book club since he'd already committed to that, plus some new ladies had booked in based on him being there. It was only fair.

What wasn't fair was that he hadn't told Noelle he was leaving at the end of the week when the next stagecoach came through Dewberry. Buying his ticket meant Howie couldn't change his mind. Or if he did, he'd lose his money. He wasn't a miser, but he hated throwing money away.

"You already know some of our parishioners," she continued, "from book club. Let me introduce you to our preacher." She turned and he studied her profile. No matter which way he looked at her, she was the most beautiful creature he'd ever set eyes on. Still, he might be biased.

Her hair was a darker brown than his, and when he looked into her eyes, it was like looking into a mirror. Her eyes were a dark chocolate brown, not unlike his own. It got him to wondering what their children would be like.

Howie's heart pounded. Where was his mind running? It was absolutely crazy to think this way when he knew he was leaving at the end of the week. He was getting far too close to Noelle Jenkins and it had to end. She had her life, and he had his, but without her in it…would he be happy? That was the question he'd been pondering for days, and the reason he'd decided to leave. He was already in far too deep and was having trouble pulling himself out.

"Howie, I'd like you to meet Preacher Abraham Flannery. Preacher, this is Howie Jones."

He reached out and shook the preacher's hand. "Pleased to meet you, Preacher Flannery. Your sermon today was inspiring."

"I'm happy to meet you, Mr. Jones. I've heard quite a bit about you. Are you staying long?"

Howie was now in a predicament. He couldn't lie to the preacher, so he had to choose his words carefully. He didn't want Noelle to find out from anyone else. "I doubt I'll be here much longer. My book is close to finished."

"Dewberry is a delightful place, and the people are wonderful." Was the preacher trying to convince him to stay?

"They certainly are," Howie said, glancing sideways at Noelle. His entire body filled with warmth and he wondered why he was even considering leaving. There was so much going for him here in Dewberry.

"Do you think you'll settle down here?" The preacher's question was one he'd already asked himself. Could he settle in Dewberry? There was a lot riding on that question, but Howie was fairly certain the answer was no. Which made it even more imperative he leave at the end of the week.

"Honestly? I don't know. I haven't been here long enough to even ponder such a situation." When he glanced at Noelle, she was on the other side of the hall, chatting to Mrs. Grayson. She didn't know he was even considering leaving so soon.

The preacher nodded and they were interrupted by another parishioner. Howie left them to it. Somewhere in all the chaos that was the after church meet-up, he was handed a cup of coffee. He glanced up, and Noelle stood in front of him, a smile on her face. "Black and strong; exactly how you like it." She led him to a corner at the back of the hall where they could sit and talk without the noise of one hundred people drowning them out.

He was in his element here. People from all walks of life congregated here, likely on a weekly basis. Back home, three times this number came to the weekly service, and despite his attending there for several years, he didn't know anyone. Not really. After only a short time here in Dewberry, he already knew a handful of people. Life here was completely different to Helena.

When he'd arrived, Howie hated it – Dewberry was far too quiet for his liking. Now that he'd come to know the place and the people better, he was rather enjoying it. When he spent time with Noelle, it felt as though his life had more meaning. When he was in her little store writing, it was as though he was wrapped up in her warmth…and her love. He felt more at home there than he felt in his own little cottage back in Helena. The more he thought about it, the crazier it sounded. They'd known each other such a short period of time, he found it difficult to believe either one of them could love the other. If he didn't know better, he'd swear he was falling for the modest bookstore owner.

What if he decided to stay longer instead of rushing into a decision that he might regret? More than likely, he would regret it, he was almost certain. But on the other hand, would he find himself in too deep if he stayed?

Howie had some important decisions to make. His heart felt as though it was pulling him in different directions.

"I enjoy being with you," Noelle said out of the blue as they strolled home from church. It was true, she felt happier and more joyful with Howie around. She glanced up as it began to snow again and giggled like a schoolgirl.

Howie chuckled and tickled her under the chin. "I feel the same way." He stopped to study her more closely and stared into her eyes. "I have no idea how long I'll be here," he said carefully. "Try not to get used to me being around." His eyes looked sad as he spoke.

It was a strange thing for him to say, but nonetheless, it made her heart thud. She didn't want to think about a time when he might not be around anymore. She'd become quite accustomed to him being in *Book Time* every day, just as she'd gotten used to sharing his break times. They suited each other well. At least Noelle thought so.

She felt comforted and protected with him around, which sounded strange because she had nothing to be protected from. There was also a subtle calmness about him. He was good with people, and not once had he refused to chat with her customers despite trying to work on a book. Most of the time, she didn't know he was there, but when she glanced up from what she was doing, there he was, sitting by the fire, head down and writing. It was like a giant hug enveloping her, and it made her feel good.

"Why don't we go for a drive this afternoon?" Howie's words were unexpected, but she liked the idea. "I could hire a buggy and you could show me around."

"It sounds nice, but the livery is closed today."

Howie sighed. "Let me try anyway. I have a way of convincing people, at least some of the time." It was true; Howie was a very persuasive man, usually without trying.

Excitement spread through her. What a lovely way to spend an afternoon – just her and Howie. Hopefully, the snow kept away, for a few hours at least. They strolled to the livery together, and he went up to the residence, leaving Noelle to wait downstairs. Old man Garner came out and didn't look too pleased. Until Howie pulled out a wad of notes and handed them over. Then he was elated.

"Let's have something to eat while the livery owner gets the buggy ready." She had no idea what he'd said to Horace Garner, but it obviously worked. As they always said, money talks, and Garner loved money.

Howie guided her toward *Ma's Kitchen*. Apart from the *Dewberry Hotel*, the diner was the only eatery open on a Sunday afternoon. She could have prepared something, but that wouldn't be proper.

"We don't have a lot of time," he told Merry, the diner's owner, and she suggested hearty beef soup with hot rolls.

"My goodness, your food is good," he told Merry as he paid when they were leaving. He also left a small tip. "I wish there was somewhere like this back home." He smiled, then his smile was gone as quickly as it came. It had Noelle baffled.

"It was delicious as always, Merry," Noelle said as she pulled on her thick coat and gloves. She turned to Howie. "We'd better get moving. Old man Garner is not a patient man, as we know." Merry grinned but didn't say a word.

Howie hurried her out the door, and the cold air hit her in the face. The weather was only going to get worse the closer they got to Christmas. At least by going today the snow wasn't heavy. Give it another week, maybe less, and it would be so thick they'd barely see an arm's length in front of them.

The horse and buggy were waiting when they returned. Noelle had no idea how much he'd paid the old man, but Garner was the most pleasant Noelle had ever known him to be. She suspected money had to be a factor.

Howie helped her up, and she relished the feel of his hands on her waist. Too bad they had an audience; otherwise, she might have savored the moment. There was a thick blanket on the seat, which was a blessed relief. The cold was beginning to leach into her bones. Howie was given a few instructions about the rig and how to get to various places then he climbed up onto the buggy. He spread the blanket to cover them both then scooted closer to Noelle to ensure they were both fully covered. His warmth seeped into her and she appreciated it.

Howie lifted the reins and they were soon on the move. She watched his every move, and her heart thudded. Noelle hadn't been this close to him before; hadn't been this close to any man before. He turned to face her. "You all right there? You seem a little…intense. Worried even."

Worried? No, she wasn't worried, but this was all new to her. Of course, she'd ridden a buggy before, but that was with her father, not a man she wasn't married to. "I'm fine," she said quietly, and he studied her.

"Are you sure? You don't seem to be yourself." He turned back to face the road, concentrating on where he was going. He was the one who seemed intense. "Horace told me a few good places we could visit. I hope you don't mind."

So it was Horace, was it? She'd known the man his entire life and had never been invited to call him by his first name. "Not at all. It's nice to get out for a change."

"It is, isn't it?" He faced her again, and he seemed more relaxed now, which was exactly how she now felt. Being away from Dewberry had a strange effect on her. When she was there, even at home, Noelle felt she needed to be doing something – for the shop, her customers, and even in her little cottage. Up here in the hills was different. She was too far away to be able to do anything, even if she wanted to.

Noelle leaned back and took in the scenery. It truly was beautiful up here. The trees were covered in smatterings of snow, and it looked like a fairytale. They were perfect, and not unlike the small trees the business owners often displayed in their stores along Dewberry Lane.

It wasn't long until Howie was slowing the buggy. "Here we are," he said, pulling the handle on the brake and jumping down. He secured the horse then came around to the side to help her down. She again relished the moment his hands came to her waist. He stared up into her eyes and slowly brought her to the ground, ensuring she didn't slip on the slurry scattered about.

"It is so beautiful," she said as she glanced around them. She couldn't curtail the excitement she was feeling. "I don't believe I've been here before."

He reached out and took her hands in his. "I'm glad. We can experience it together." As they stood there together, not another soul around, calmness filled her. It surprised her since Noelle worried about being alone with Howie. Not that she thought he'd hurt her or take advantage in any way; it was that she'd never been alone with a man before. Not anywhere remote or isolated like this, anyway.

She hooked her arm in his, and they wandered about, checking out the area surrounding the small clearing where Howie had tied the buggy. "It's like we've stumbled on a whole different world," she said quietly, all the while taking it all in.

"It is rather beautiful," he told her. "just like you." He stood in front of her and pulled her closer. Noelle looked up into his eyes.

"I'm not…"

He leaned in and kissed her, interrupting her protest. "You are the most beautiful woman I have ever encountered," he said when he came up for air. Then he kissed her again.

Noelle sighed. She was falling for him, and knew she shouldn't. By his own admission, Howie could leave Dewberry at any moment. Once his book was finished, he'd probably leave both the town and her.

For now, she would relish his kisses and cherish being held by him. She would not let this day be spoiled by the fact they were soulmates who could never be together.

Chapter Five

After roaming around for about thirty minutes, checking the area out, they decided to move on. Howie helped her up onto the buggy. His hands around her waist sent a shiver up Noelle's spine, and she wondered how she would feel once he was gone from Dewberry.

She had been fighting her emotions for far too long, but now was not the time to renege. By his own admission, Howie would be leaving Dewberry in the not-too-distant future. She had to keep her distance from him, both physically and emotionally. If she didn't, then her heart would be crushed.

She studied him as he climbed back up on the buggy. "Horace says we mustn't miss the Dewberry Falls. Have you seen them?" He turned to her, waiting for an answer before he continued. Just the thought of it sent a shiver down her spine. It was cold up there because of the waterfall, but for Howie, she would endure it.

"I have been there, but it was years ago. When I was a small child and my parents were still alive." She pulled the blanket up further, trying to keep out the cold before it got worse. "It can be quite chilly up there."

He stared at her momentarily. "Perhaps we'd best not go." He flicked the reins, and the buggy began to move.

"No, please," she said, pleading in her voice. "I wasn't trying to deter you. It's a beautiful place. I'd hate for you to miss out on seeing it." After all, once he was gone from Dewberry, there would be no other chances.

He smiled at her then caressed her cheek with one hand, the other still on the reins. "If you're certain?"

She really wasn't. The further away from town they got, the less they complied with propriety. But it was too late to think about that. They'd been alone and isolated for well over an hour now. "Do you know where to go?" She studied his profile as he drove the buggy forward.

"Horace gave me specific instructions." He smiled at her then faced forward again. She'd warned him the terrain could be treacherous in places, so he needed to keep his eyes on the road. They continued in silence until they came to a fork in the road. It was then Howie looked uncertain.

"Take the road to the right," she said quietly. He nodded and continued.

"We must be close," Howie said after a while. "I can hear the roar of the falls. I guess it won't be long now." He turned to her and grinned.

"They're literally around the corner," she said, her heart thudding. This place brought back so many memories of her childhood. Of her parents, now gone.

His eyes were only off the road momentarily, but it was long enough. Before she realized what was happening, Noelle found herself being flung out of the buggy and onto the road.

"Noelle," he shouted then jumped down from the buggy in a panic. The wretched contraption had tossed her to the ground like a rag doll.

He ran to her side where she lay in the ditch that had caused the accident. Only it wasn't an accident – he'd become far too complacent and was drinking in the beauty that was Noelle every chance he got. She'd warned him about the precarious state of the roads, but he hadn't listened. And now she'd been injured. How badly was yet to be known. How he wished that was him in her place.

She lay on her side with her eyes closed. Her long brown hair was messed up, and her gown was covered in dirt. Snow and slush surrounded her. He crouched down next her, his heart pounding. Had he killed her? He reached out to touch her and Noelle's eyes fluttered opened. She stared up at him in confusion. His relief was palpable, but it in no way indemnified him from his negligence.

"What happened?" Her voice was full of confusion, and his heart was full of concern. What if he'd killed her? He suddenly felt hollow. *What if he had killed her?* He would never have forgiven himself. He had known her such a short time, and yet felt incredibly close to her. He stared down into her face. It was bloodied and bruised.

He did that to her. It was totally his fault.

She blinked a few times as though trying to get her bearings. "Stay there a moment," he said then put his arm around her back. "I'm going to help you to your feet. Don't move until I say so."

Noelle nodded but still looked bewildered. She'd had a bump to the head, no doubt, so her confusion was understandable. "Ready?" She nodded and he helped her up. She winced as her right foot hit the ground. *Had she broken it?*

It was then he realized he hadn't thought this through. The buggy was down a ditch; where would he place her? He glanced about and found a log to prop her on until he could right their transportation. Her clothes were partially wet from the snow, and she was shivering. Whether from shock or cold, Howie wasn't certain.

Grabbing the blanket from the buggy, he wrapped it around her. "Stay there while I get the buggy out of the ditch." She nodded and pulled the blanket tighter around herself. The horse came through it all virtually unscathed, but the buggy, unfortunately, did not. One wheel was buckled to the extent they couldn't return home with it. He pulled the buggy out of the ditch and away from further incident. Howie unhitched the horse and tied it to a nearby tree. What they would do now, he wasn't sure.

With darkness surrounding them, Noelle huddled up against Howie in the lopsided buggy. The thick blanket covered them both, and she leaned with her back against Howie's chest. Her clothes had all but dried out, and she was no longer shivering, but her ankle was throbbing.

Howie insisted it might be broken, but Noelle could still wiggle her toes, so she thought not. She'd made him turn around while she ripped a make-shift bandage from her petticoat, then he'd wrapped it for her. As his fingers held her ankle sturdy, bolts of lightening went through her. She knew it was wrong for him to touch her that way, but there was no other choice. She'd been in an incredible amount of pain; the makeshift bandage had helped alleviate the pain.

On second thought, perhaps Howie was right. The last thing she needed now was a broken ankle. How would she run her business? How would she get to work and home again each night? The potential problems were insurmountable.

"Do you think they'll send a search party?"

Howie's voice was full of regret, and she tilted her head to glance back at him. "Not tonight. It's too dark, and we know how bad the roads up here are in daylight. They're far more dangerous at night."

"Of course, you're right," he said quietly. Was he thinking of the implications of them spending the night together? The fact it was unavoidable and was totally innocent meant nothing. The people of Dewberry would have a field day once they were rescued and returned home. She shivered at the thought. Noelle didn't want to marry Howie. Not that he wanted to marry her, but the last thing she wanted was a forced marriage. If she married, it would be for love.

That sent her thoughts in an entirely different direction. Did she love Howie? She certainly felt something for him, but she wasn't sure it was love. She was almost positive Howie felt nothing for her.

If he did, he wouldn't be planning to leave, and he'd already admitted it would happen in the near future. Noelle sighed at the thought of it all. Life was far too complicated.

His arms came up around her from under the blanket and it startled her. "Sorry, I didn't mean to scare you. I was trying to keep you warm. You're shivering."

She was, it was true. But she was no longer cold, Howie had seen to that. "Don't apologize. I was simply lost in my thoughts." She tilted her head back and glanced up at him. "I can feel the warmth coming from you." She knew it was wrong the moment Howie suggested they huddle together to conserve each other's body warmth. In essence, she had none and was shivering. He was giving away his warmth to her, and she gave nothing in exchange.

"I'm truly sorry," he whispered in the darkness. "This wasn't the way I'd planned our day. I can't even blame the state of the buggy." He pulled her a little closer. "It was due to my stupidity. I'll never forgive myself."

She felt his body stiffen against her and lifted a hand to cover his. "There's nothing to forgive. We're both in one piece, and tomorrow morning we'll be rescued. I can guarantee it."

"Oh, but we're not. Your ankle…"

"Is fine. Perhaps a little battered, but I will survive." She stared up into the murky sky. The moon was hiding behind the clouds and barely visible. Apart from Howie's breathing, it was quiet. Almost too quiet, and she wondered what lay out there where they couldn't see. She shuffled closer to Howie. "Are you scared?" Her words were soft, full of emotion.

"I promise to keep you safe," he whispered, a modicum of mirth in his voice. She shuffled even closer, and he held her more tightly than before. Noelle closed her eyes and was soon asleep.

Howie lay quietly, listening to the birds and other forest creatures begin their day. Noelle was still asleep, her breathing quiet and steady. She was snuggled close to him, and he reveled in it, all the time knowing he shouldn't. His arms were still around her, the blanket pulled up to her chin. Thank goodness Horace Garner has supplied a blanket for them, otherwise, who knew what could have happened.

She suddenly wiggled about and her head leaned against his chest in an almost intimate way. Howie knew it was wrong, but he had no intention of disturbing her sleep. He'd prayed long and hard during the night for her to be safe. He swallowed back the lump in his throat at the thought of what might have happened. Had there been a rock where she landed, Noelle could be dead right now. He tightened his grip, trying to reassure himself she was truly all right.

He'd enjoyed watching the sunrise from up here in the mountains; it was spectacular. But he lamented they hadn't made it to the waterfall. Perhaps they'd visit some other time. But he knew that wouldn't happen. Howie would be back in Helena soon, so seeing the waterfall was now out of the question.

He leaned back into the buggy and relaxed. There was nothing to do until the search party arrived. Horace would have surely put out alarm bells by now, and he guessed it wouldn't be long before they left town to find what had happened.

As if on cue, he heard voices, then the sounds of horses rounding the corner. The very same corner where he had lost his footing on the road and landed Noelle in a precarious situation. He glanced up as they got closer.

Noelle stirred as he softly shook her, trying to bring her out of sleep gently. Suddenly, she stared up at him, her eyes opened wide. "Oh my!" she said as more than a dozen horses and wagons came around the bend, the sheriff and deputy leading the entourage. Horace Garner was amongst the rescuers.

Howie straightened, his whole body stiffening. Noelle's reaction was no different. "Stay here," he whispered to her and climbed out of the buggy to face the music.

"Morning, Sheriff," Howie said, only Sheriff Jack Dawson didn't look too pleased.

"You all right, Miss Jenkins?"

"She's fine, except for an injured ankle," Howie responded.

Deputy Hank Grogan stepped forward and pushed against Howie's chest. "The sheriff wasn't asking you," he growled then stormed toward Noelle. Did they think...? Howie's heart thudded. He would never harm Noelle, or any other woman.

"Look here. If you're insinuating..." But he didn't get to finish the sentence.

"Not a word, Jones," the sheriff demanded. "Stand over there until I tell you otherwise." His scowl was enough for Howie; he did as he was told.

Doc Wigham rushed forward and checked Noelle over. "A few cuts and bruises, which are easy to fix, but looks like her ankle is badly sprained." He went to lift her out of the damaged buggy, and Howie protested.

"I can do that," he said, feeling irritated, which surprised him as he wasn't sure why. He stepped back when the deputy put a hand to Howie's chest.

Horace checked the buggy over. "Here's the problem," he said loudly so all could hear. "What did you do? Go off the road?"

That's exactly what he did. "I must have gotten too close to the edge and the wheel slipped over the side."

"Luckily, I brought another wheel with me. I figured that would be the problem." He walked over to Howie and leaned in. "You've put yourself in a pot of hot water, Son," he said quietly then quickly walked off.

Howie swallowed. Did that mean what he thought it meant? He had a feeling he wouldn't be going anywhere anytime soon.

Chapter Six

By the time they arrived back in Dewberry, Noelle's stomach was rumbling. It had been quite some time since she'd eaten. Howie was in the same boat, but he'd been forced to travel with the sheriff and deputy, and no one would let her talk to him.

She rode back with Doc Wigham, who was over cautious about her ankle. He was almost certain it wasn't broken, as she had been, but needed to have a better look once they arrived in town. She kept her eyes on Howie and felt sorry for him. Noelle was certain he was under duress, especially being sandwiched between the two lawmen. Why everyone assumed she'd been compromised was beyond her. But even if she had been, wasn't it her choice? She wasn't a child after all, and as a twenty-six-year-old spinster, she got to make her own decisions. Didn't she?

By the time they arrived back in Dewberry, her sympathy for Howie had turned to anger against the men who had come to rescue them. Who did they think they were, throwing judgement on Howie and her? They'd gone out for a pleasant afternoon's drive and ended up being stuck. There was nothing more to it, and they shouldn't go around throwing aspersions on Howie's reputation. Or hers for that matter.

Arriving at the doctor's clinic, she tried to climb down off the buggy, but the pain in her ankle stopped her. The trip down the bumpy roads had done nothing to appease her discomfort, and had in fact, made it far worse. Her mind kept clicking over with worse case scenarios. What if she couldn't work? Her biggest worry being how she would physically get there. Putting her foot to the ground caused unspoken agony, so what hope did she have of walking all the way from home to the bookstore?

"What happens now?" Doc Wigham's head shot up as he lifted her from the buggy and carried her into the clinic.

"I'll give you a thorough checking over then I might be able to answer that question." He smiled at her, the sort of smile she'd seen him use before when he wanted to reassure an ill patient. "I don't think your ankle is broken, so don't worry yourself about that."

Her ankle was the least of her worries. What really concerned her was Howie. What were they doing to him? What sort of duress were they putting him under? It made her heart ache just thinking about the possibilities. "Is Howie all right?" Her voice was quiet and full of emotion. She didn't recognize it as her own.

As she sat on the bed in the doctor's office, her ankle in his hands, he glanced up at her. "Mr. Jones is a grown man. I'm sure he can look after himself."

Noelle wasn't so certain, and tears filled her eyes. "We didn't do anything wrong." The words came out almost as a wail, and before she knew it, tears were rolling down her face. "We just went for a drive and then there was an accident. None of this was Howie's fault." She brushed her fingers across her wet cheeks and tried to compose herself. Why couldn't people just mind their own business?

After bandaging her swollen ankle, the doc began work on her face. He had a bowl of warm soapy water and a face cloth and began to dab at her face. "This will sting a little, but we need to clean it up. You have a nasty bruise on your cheekbone too."

Noelle hated to think what she looked like, but it too would heal. Suddenly, the door burst open and Howie came rushing in. "Are you all right? Is it broken?" He glanced down frantically at her bandaged foot.

"It is not broken, and you need to leave, Mr. Jones." Doc Wigham was quite stern in his dealings with Howie. Noelle had not seen him that way before. "Please leave so I can care for my patient, or I will be forced to call the sheriff."

"No! I want him to stay." Noelle was confused. What was going on, and why was everyone treating Howie this way? He had literally saved her, and they were treating him like the enemy. It wasn't fair.

The doctor threw Howie a look that said you can stay, but only because my patient wants you to. He finished his examination then left the pair alone, but with the door open. Howie stepped toward Noelle and wrapped his arms around her.

"I'm sorry, I truly am," he said, not for the first time since the accident. "I would take it all back if I could." He stared into her eyes, and it gave her the opportunity to study him. He looked tired. And stressed.

"You do know I am fine?" Her arms went up his back and she hugged him back. "A little inconvenience with the ankle, but apart from that…"

His fingers caressed her face. "Cuts and bruises have marred your beautiful face. I'm—"

"—Will you stop saying that?" Now she was cross. Little damage had been done, and they would soon be able to go back to their normal lives.

He stared at her then furrowed his brows. "Have you not heard? I have ruined your reputation in this town, and now we must wed." Noelle's heart pounded. They were being forced to marry? By whom? She sat rigid; this was not right. Why should they comply with the expectations of other people? She had a store to run, and Howie had his writing to worry about.

"They can't force us," she said between gritted teeth.

He stared deep into her eyes. His face was full of sympathy. "I cannot allow your reputation to be left in tatters. You will never recover from it. What man wants to marry a woman of dubious scruples?"

He lifted her hands and brought them to his lips. "I won't do that to you, so we will be wed." He glanced up at her. His next words were softly said. "It's happening later today."

Noelle felt anger rise up through her whole being. How dare they? Who did those men think they were? They'd not done anything wrong; Howie had been the perfect gentleman and had protected her the entire time. And this is how his chivalry was repaid? It made her heart ache. If they married, everyone would say it was forced, which it was. If they didn't wed, Howie would be forever sullied for not doing the right thing. And she would be branded a harlot. No matter what they did, they couldn't win.

She buried her face in his chest and wished for the innocent days of their past.

"Are you ready, Miss Jenkins?" Mrs. Grayson stood staunchly beside her. If it weren't for the old dear, Noelle knew she wouldn't be here now. Well, she might be here, but not looking her best. That was if you called battered and bruised her best.

What Mrs. Grayson did was ensure she had something decent to wear; something worthy of a wedding ceremony, even one that was hurriedly put together. Noelle didn't, so it was arranged for her. She'd commandeered Ivy from *Buttons and Bows*, and between them, they'd come up with a beautiful peach-colored gown that she was proud to wear down the aisle. Too bad about the crutches she had to maneuver on the way.

Howie stood at the front of the church, waiting for his bride. He looked splendid in his sleek black suit and glanced over his shoulder at her. He winced with every step she took, and Noelle was certain she only had to say the word and he'd scoop her up and carry her down the aisle to her destination. She certainly felt like tossing the crutches aside and letting him be her knight in shining armor, but that would never do. He'd already come to her rescue – twice in the past twenty-four hours – she couldn't ask him to do it yet again.

"Take a break if you need to, my dear." Mrs. Grayson's words were meant to be reassuring, Noelle was certain, but they only reconfirmed her painful and desperate situation. Her head was filled with what-ifs and how they would move forward from this.

She didn't want to marry Howie, and she was certain he didn't want to marry her. So why were they doing this? Why did they let annoying old men force their hands and make them comply? Her chin quivered and she knew it was all too much. She glanced about and seated herself on one of the nearby pews. She was exhausted and she wasn't even halfway there.

Howie rushed to her side, oblivious to the protests from Mrs. Grayson and the preacher. Sheriff Dawson was their other witness, wanting to ensure the ceremony went as planned, no doubt.

"It will be all right," Howie whispered as he slid his arm under her and lifted her up. He carried Noelle to the front of the church and sat her on the front pew. He'd always been attuned to her feelings and thoughts, and today was no different.

"Dearly beloved," Preacher Flannery began.

Very soon, the ceremony was over and the marriage certificate signed. As she stared down at the document in her hands, Noelle reflected how their afternoon sojourn had turned into such a disaster.

Deputy Grogan watched as Howie moved his belongings from the Dewberry Hotel into Noelle's cottage. Howie had thought a marriage in name only was appropriate in the circumstances – he would continue living at the hotel and Noelle would continue living in her cottage. But it wasn't to be. The lawman, and apparently everyone else in town, decided they should have a real marriage and not a sham one.

Noelle was huddled next to the fire in what he discovered was her favorite chair with her foot elevated. She sat in silence as Howie's belongings were brought into her neat little cottage. She'd said little about their situation, and he didn't press her about it. There would be a time, but that wasn't now.

She'd told him to make himself at home, since it would be his home too from now on. He wasn't sure how she felt about that.

Howie wandered about, checking the place out. There was a main bedroom with a double bed, and two spare rooms. Each of those rooms held a single bed already made up, ready for use. One also held a desk and chair. The kitchen was small; big enough for one person to cook at any given time. A small wooden table covered with a red and white gingham tablecloth sat to one side. In the center sat a small vase of flowers, and surrounding the table were three chairs. A modern bathroom was nearby. When he went inside, Howie noticed it had running water, which surprised him.

"I need to open the bookstore," Noelle told him as he re-entered the sitting room. "My customers will be wondering why the store is closed on a Monday."

That made Howie chuckle. He was certain the entire township of Dewberry would have heard they'd been forced to marry by a bunch of do-gooders who couldn't mind their own business. Instead of saying the words out loud, he reassured his new wife all would be fine. "I can go and open the bookstore."

She squeezed her eyes closed, and he heard her sigh before she opened them again. "Thank you, but you don't know what needs to be done, or even how to do it. I need to go there and do it myself."

He stiffened at the thought. "How do you propose to do that? You can't walk on that foot. Besides, it's too far."

"I can do what I want," she said defiantly, her chin lifting as she spoke.

He could see what was happening. She was retaliating because they'd been forced into marriage despite neither of them doing anything wrong. Unless you count enjoying the company of a beautiful woman because that's all that had happened.

"We'll work something out." He picked up the few belongings he'd brought with him to Dewberry and headed toward one of the spare rooms.

"Put your things on the bed," she called. "We'll put them away later." He chose the room closest to Noelle's since there was a small desk there he could utilize. He returned for his notepads and placed them on the desk. This room had a large window near the desk, so he would also have the benefit of natural light.

He couldn't help but think if this had been a real marriage, he'd be storing his belongings in the main bedroom and would spend his nights with his wife. Perhaps that's what he should have done anyway, but that would be rather presumptuous of him. Since this was to be a marriage in name only, nothing had changed except his living quarters. Everything had happened in such a whirlwind he wasn't sure how he felt. But he did know he had feelings for Noelle. Had they been left to their own devices those feelings may have grown. Now they'd been pushed into a very tight corner, things may never change for them.

He only had to look at Noelle to know how upset she was over the entire situation. He was too, but at least he could get around when he wanted to. Doc Wigham said she'd be off her foot for at least a few days. She was already frustrated by the fact, and he would do whatever he could to help make it easier on her.

Howie's stomach rumbled, reminding him supper time was nearly upon them. He checked the pantry, only to discover it was near empty – there were half a dozen eggs, an open packet of flour, and half a loaf of bread. The icebox held a piece of thick bacon, a chunk of butter, and almost a pint of milk. That was supper sorted, but tomorrow, he would visit the mercantile.

The kettle boiled and he made two coffees. They needed to talk, and now was the perfect opportunity. Rummaging through the cupboards, he found a tin with a handful of cookies in it. He added those to a small plate. He placed them all on a tray and carried them into the sitting room. Entertaining was not his forte, nor did he enjoy it, but now he was Noelle's husband, so it wasn't really entertaining. Was it?

Closing the distance between the kitchen and the sitting room felt like the longest walk in history. Neither of them had foreseen what had transpired, and neither had wanted it. Noelle, who was now his wife, had a thriving business and did not need his interference. On the other hand, he could write just about anywhere depending on the noise level. It was far easier to live in Helena where his publisher was based, but that choice had now been taken away from him.

"I'm sorry…" he began as he lowered the tray to the small side table. But Noelle spoke at the same time, speaking almost the same words. She glanced up at him momentarily then lowered her eyes to her hands that were twisting in her laps. She pulled her lips into a tight line.

He handed her a mug of hot coffee. "You have nothing to be sorry for," he said, passing her the plate of cookies. She glanced down at them.

"I'm nearly…" She stopped then took a deep breath and let it out slowly. "*We're* nearly out of supplies. I would have normally replenished my pantry today."

It would take time for both of them to get used to the new situation. "I can do that. Tomorrow, I'll open the bookstore. No point in you losing customers when I can keep things running." He smiled tentatively, and she stared at him with sad eyes.

He'd often wondered what life as a married man would be like. This was far from what he'd imagined. When Howie had come to Dewberry for a short visit, little did he know how dramatically his life would change.

Chapter Seven

Supper of pancakes with a side of bacon was delicious. Noelle would never have guessed Howie could cook, let alone cook well. Most of the bachelors she knew ate out most of the time, but apparently, that wasn't her new husband. It seemed he could handle himself quite well in the kitchen.

Today had been a memorable day for them both, and not in a good way. She'd hoped it was all a nightmare, and she'd wake up to find it wasn't real. So far that hadn't happened, and her throbbing ankle reminded her of that fact constantly. "Supper was lovely. Thank you," she said quietly. When she looked up, he was studying her. "Is something wrong, Howie?"

"You're in pain. It's written all over your face." He was right, she was in pain, but she couldn't have supper in the sitting room like he'd suggested. That wouldn't be right. "Doc Wigham said you needed to keep your ankle elevated to stop the pain." He stood and headed to the countertop where he'd already dished up cold apple pie leftovers. "I'm sorry there's no cream, but I will get some tomorrow."

He was trying so hard, maybe too hard, to do his best to look after her. Placing the bowls on the table, he handed her a spoon. "Eat up, and then you can elevate your leg again. Or better still, do that first, and we'll eat in the sitting room."

She screwed her nose up at him. As much as his suggestion sounded far more sensible, eating somewhere other than the kitchen was not something she did. Before she had an opportunity to answer, he came around to her and slid his arm underneath her, then picked Noelle up.

"Hey!" He ignored her protests and carried her back into the sitting room. He might be bigger and stronger than her, but it didn't mean he got to make decisions for her.

He placed her gently onto her favorite chair next to the fire. Howie tenderly lifted her leg and placed her ankle on the elevation, as it was before. He fussed about covering her with a blanket then left the room. His heart was in the right place, but now she was fuming. Was this what marriage to Howie would be like? Him making all the decisions, whether she agreed or not? Heat rose through her at the very thought of her independence being taken away from her.

All of this because they'd decided to take an afternoon drive. What sort of stupidity was this?

Her thoughts were interrupted when Howie handed her the bowl of apple pie. When she looked down, she noticed the spoon was still tightly gripped in her hand.

"What's wrong?" He stood over her, frowning. He always could read her thoughts.

"You are not in charge of me," she said boldly then wanted to take it back. He was her husband after all, but only because…she didn't want to think about it anymore.

He sat on the chair next to her and held her hand. "I know that," he said quietly. "This is going to be a learning period for us both. Neither of us asked for this, but it's happened, and we have to deal with it."

Howie was right, of course he was, but that didn't make it any easier. She glanced down at the apple pie he'd handed her. She didn't have much of an appetite tonight, but she really needed to eat. They'd both missed meals lately, and it wasn't good for either one of them. She said nothing, and he reached over and put his fingers to her chin, forcing her gaze to him. He had a sadness about him, much the way she felt.

She stared into his face momentarily then nodded slightly. He relaxed his grip then let her go. "I know," she said quietly, then began eating. There was nothing else to say. They'd been placed in a situation neither of them relished, and now they had to deal with it, like it or not.

It seemed like hours later when it was time for bed. The atmosphere between them was awkward, which wasn't surprising given their situation. Howie carried her to the bathroom to allow her to freshen up before bed. Knowing he was hovering outside the door, waiting for her, didn't ease her mind. She carried out her ablutions as quickly as possible then hobbled to the door. To her dismay, he scooped her up and carried Noelle to bed. Her heart fluttered at the thought.

"Can you help me," she asked quietly, indicating her nightgown that was out of reach. He silently passed the nightgown to her. As she sat on the side of the bed, Noelle wasn't sure what to expect. Neither of them had discussed their wedding night; it wasn't really a subject easily talked about.

"Do you need help removing your dress?" Perhaps in other circumstances, but these were far from normal conditions. She shook her head and he nodded. "Then I shall bid you goodnight. Unless you need further assistance?"

Noelle stared at him. He wasn't sleeping in her bed?

The door closed quietly behind him, and she wasn't sure what to think. After all the time they'd spent together, the good times they'd enjoyed, and discussions they'd undertaken over the past weeks, she thought she knew Howie well. How could she only now be finding out the truth? That she actually repulsed him.

Howie lay in bed staring up at the ceiling. Leaving Noelle alone in her bedroom was the hardest thing he'd ever had to do. When he glanced back as he closed the door, she was close to tears. It had taken all his effort not to run back to her and envelope her in his arms. He'd known he was in love with her for some time now, but his feelings weren't reciprocated, and he would never force himself on her. Just because they'd been forced to marry didn't mean they would have an intimate relationship. It meant they would live under the same roof and nothing more.

If Noelle had loved him back, it would be a different situation all together, but she'd given no indication of any such thing. Even when he'd kissed her yesterday on that fateful trip, she hadn't indicated an interest in him. Until she told him otherwise, he would sleep in the spare room and would keep his distance. He wouldn't make advances towards her, and as difficult as it would be, he wouldn't kiss her. Not unless she gave him permission.

He'd tossed and turned for some hours now and sleep had continued to elude him. Instead of continuing down this path, Howie climbed out of bed and lit the lantern. Between that and the moonlight shining through the window, there would be enough light for him to write. Might as well do something productive rather than to stare at the ceiling the entire night.

The hardest part was knowing Noelle was on the other side of the door, and was totally out of his reach. He wondered how long before the situation would change. Or perhaps it never would.

His heart thudded. If that were the case, he might as well leave Dewberry. She could seek an annulment if that's what she wanted, or they could stay married but live separately. Their marriage had saved her reputation, and right now, that's all that mattered.

Shoulders slumped, he sat down at the beautifully built desk and began work on his book. But his heart wasn't in it, and his concentration was shot. All he wanted to do right now was storm through that door and hold his wife in his arms. Once he did that, he knew he would never let her go.

Howie was up and about, no doubt preparing breakfast. Noelle could hear him moving around, but so far, he'd not come to her room. She'd tossed and turned most of the night, resulting in little sleep, and she was certain there would be black circles under her eyes.

The saddest part about all of this was before the forced marriage, they'd been enjoying each other's company. But now there was a barrier between them that Noelle wasn't certain they'd ever break down. Why did people have to interfere in their lives? Even Mrs. Grayson, whom she'd known forever, thought this was the best solution, even if she did have her doubts about Howie at the beginning.

He'd proven himself to Mrs. Grayson and the townsfolk, and then they'd turned on both of them. To be fair, not everyone was involved, but rather a handful of elders and those in authority. Noelle sat up in bed and it took all her effort not to cry at the mess she now found herself in. But crying had never helped anyone. It made her feel better for a while, but left her with swollen and blotchy eyes and a red face. That was the last thing she wanted. Even if Howie didn't want her in that way, she still didn't want him to see her at her worst.

Besides, crying was not going to fix anything and would give her a headache. She had too much to do today for that to happen. She slid her legs out of the bed, being extra careful about her sprained ankle. She thanked God for sparing her from a broken ankle; a sprain was certainly better. But now she had to solve the issue of how she would get to work.

She was in the process of getting out of bed when she heard a light tap at her bedroom door. "Come in," she called then quickly pulled the blankets up around herself. Howie might be her husband, but since he'd chosen not to consummate their marriage, he was not entitled to any husbandly rights.

He stood there in the doorway, looking every bit as bad as she felt. He'd obviously had an equally sleepless night as she had. "You look terrible," Noelle blurted out before she could check herself.

Howie chuckled. "You don't look so good yourself."

He was probably right. "I'm going to the bookstore today," she said forcefully. "I need to prepare for the book club later this week."

He scowled then in a low voice set her anger on fire. "That's not going to happen."

Who did he think he was? Howie couldn't tell her what to do. Well, all right, he was her husband now. But that didn't give him the right to dictate her life. She stared him down. "That's not your decision," she snapped and jumped out of bed. Excruciating pain shot from her ankle all the way up her leg, bringing tears to her eyes, and she collapsed back onto the bed.

Howie was by her side in a flash. "Take it easy," he said quietly, not so much as a skerrick of anger in his voice. He sounded far more concerned than angry. He helped her back into bed, placing a pillow under her ankle to ease her discomfort. He pulled the blankets up over her then stared down at her. "I know it's hard, but you need to rest that ankle. The more you rest it, the sooner you can get back to the store."

She had little choice and nodded her agreement.

"Good," he said quietly. "Breakfast is almost ready. I'll bring it to you shortly."

In less than twenty-four hours she had gone from being a happily single woman to married. She'd also gone from only ever eating in the kitchen to having consumed food in both her sitting room and of all places, her bedroom. If her parents could see her now, they would be fuming. They had rules, and she'd always stuck to them, even after they were gone.

She leaned back on the pile of pillows Howie had placed behind her and closed her eyes. Her life would never be the same again.

Noelle was asleep when Howie arrived back home at noon, carrying supplies he'd bought at the mercantile. She was in a lot of pain when he'd left, which could be exhausting, so he wasn't surprised she slept. Keeping as quiet as possible, he stocked the pantry after refilling the kettle. He opened an account at the mercantile and paid the little Noelle owed, closing her account down. He already knew she would be furious about that, but he wasn't about to tell her. Not yet anyway. He was her husband and was responsible for her now. That's exactly what he intended to do.

After slicing the fresh bread he'd bought, Howie made cheese sandwiches for them both. It was basic, but the best he could do under the circumstances. Besides, Noelle wouldn't want the bookstore closed for any longer than absolutely necessary.

He carried the food and coffee on a small wooden tray. He felt bad waking her up, but he was only here for a short time, and she needed to eat. Her eyes fluttered open when he entered the room, and she looked startled. Even in her disheveled state, she was beautiful. He could stand and watch her all day. But he had responsibilities, including keeping her business running smoothly while she was absent. It was, after all, his fault she was in this predicament.

He placed the tray on the chair next to her bed and fluffed the pillows for her. "How do you feel? You look better than you did this morning." He helped her sit up then placed the tray across her lap. "You've had lots of customers today – all asking after you."

She screwed up her face. "I'm sure they were. They probably wanted all the details they could get." Noelle sounded bitter, and he really couldn't blame her.

"Mrs. Grayson was the first to arrive. She was very concerned about your ankle. I assured her you are resting it, even if it is under duress." He laughed, but she wasn't amused. Quite the opposite in fact, and Howie earned himself a scowl. "Your new book club ladies came in and bought their copy of the book. They promised to read it in time."

"They would have been thrilled to see you there. After all, you're the reason they decided to attend. As it turns out, they shouldn't have bothered." She sipped her coffee, and Howie wondered if they were ever going to get past all this…unpleasantness…that had been foisted on them. "Have you eaten yet? If not, sit in here with me. It's rather lonely in here by myself."

Was she giving him a concession? It certainly felt like it. Perhaps it was the beginning of the barriers coming down. He went to the kitchen and quickly returned with his lunch. Howie would take advantage of any opportunities that came his way. At least in regard to his wife. "I sold three autographed copies of my book this morning," he said between bites. "I do have my uses after all." He glanced up at her and grinned.

She smiled but it seemed forced. "That's good. There must only be two copies left now. Of course, when your latest book is released, we must order copies of that too."

We? Was she seeing him as a partner in the store? That's not what Howie had anticipated. Nor did he want it to be that way. She owned the store in her own right, and he wouldn't take that away from her. In fact, he would insist.

"I have to leave soon. Is there anything you need before I go?" Again, that sadness to her face. Was it all due to pain, or was there another reason? He may never know.

He cleared away the tray with the empty mugs and plates then returned to the bedroom. He carried her to the bathroom then helped her back into bed. Her arms around his neck and her near naked body set his heart on fire, but Howie didn't act on any of it. Until Noelle indicated her willingness, he would not force any familiarity on her.

The hardest part was knowing that may never be the case.

Chapter Eight

After four harrowing days stuck at home alone, Noelle was finally able to attend the bookstore. Her ankle was far from normal, but the swelling had gone down, and the throbbing had eased considerably. It seemed rather ridiculous, but Howie had hired a buggy to get her to the bookstore and home again.

Tonight was book club, and she wanted to be there to oversee it. Howie had done a wonderful job organizing everything, including placing the chairs and buying supper for tonight. Despite all the goings on around them over the past days, they had both managed to finish reading *Kathleen's Burden*, which was the selected book of the week.

She pottered around in the kitchen preparing mugs for the light refreshments later tonight, while Howie sat out in the store, assisting customers. They would have a quick supper at *Ma's Kitchen*. Time would be precious, so it would likely be hearty soup and hot bread rolls; a favorite of Noelle's.

She heard the door to the store close then the click of the lock. Finally, the last customer had left. Noelle did a last-minute check – twelve mugs sat on the counter. She'd had to buy more to accommodate her newest book club members. Two dozen cupcakes were ready on the platter, and sugar, milk and spoons were all ready on the tray. She breathed a sigh of relief. How did she ever do this alone? She already knew the answer; it was always frantic, and she rarely had time to eat before her ladies arrived.

Footsteps sounded behind her, and she turned to see Howie standing in the doorway. Her heart fluttered at the sight of him there, and it was all she could do to stop herself from taking the few steps toward him and wrapping her arms around him. When she glanced up at his face, his eyes met hers and she licked her lips. A tingle went down her spine at his mere presence.

How long could they keep apart to spite other people? This was nonsense and they both knew it. She stepped forward and he did the same. She looked up into his face, and he leaned into her, enveloping her. As his hands slid up her back and into her hair that hung loose, she groaned.

"This is crazy, I am far too in love with you to keep my distance," he said, his voice husky. "May I kiss you, Mrs. Jones?"

Noelle grinned as she glanced up at him. "You certainly may, Mr. Jones."

And that's exactly what he did.

Howie unlocked the door and the book club ladies strolled in, all clutching their copy of *Kathleen's Burden*. "I've been looking forward to this all night," Mrs. Grayson said, a twinkle in her eye. Howie was certain she was, but not for the purpose of discussing the book.

Mrs. Jolimont giggled as she strolled in, and Mrs. Carson covered her mouth to try to stop him from seeing her grin. It didn't work. When they were all seated, introductions began due to the new ladies. They were locals, but rarely came to town. Everyone made them welcome, as Howie knew they would.

"What did everyone think of the book?" He could see Noelle was impatient to get underway.

"Oh, it was wonderful," said Mrs. Halliday. "Lots of mystery and surprises." She glanced at Howie and grinned as she emphasized *surprises*. Noelle rolled her eyes.

Mrs. Grayson intervened. "It was well written. Not an author I've read before, but I'd be willing to try another of her books. Speaking of books, when does your next book release, Mr. Jones?"

"Call me Howie please, everyone. My next book releases in about two months, and the next should be out in time for Christmas. I have to finish it first." Color rose in some of the ladies faces. He didn't even want to contemplate what they might be thinking. Noelle glanced across at him. Her cheeks were rosy red, so he'd guessed correctly.

The new ladies contributed to the discussion, and when they were all talked out, Noelle made coffee. Howie carried the supper tray and everyone stood around chatting.

"How is that ankle," Mrs. Grayson asked sincerely.

"It's doing fine. Thank you for asking."

"Everything back to normal now?" Knowing the older woman, there was more behind that question, but Howie wasn't getting involved. He slipped an arm around Noelle then leaned in and kissed her cheek. He felt her stiffen in his grip but knew it was because he'd been affectionate in public. He wanted nothing more than for them to be alone.

They soon chose the next week's book and everyone dispersed. It was time to tidy up and leave. Howie wanted nothing more than to abandon the tidying and go home immediately.

Noelle sat up on the buggy waiting for Howie to help her down. He'd hired the buggy for the next week, but she wasn't certain it would be needed that long. In normal circumstances, the walk to the bookstore wasn't long, but with her ankle still being tender and sore, she understood his reasoning.

He held her by the waist and lifted her gently to the ground. Noelle stared down into his face, the moonlight dancing across his features. She licked her lips as she saw him do the same, and soon he was kissing her, right there in the open. Not that anyone would see them; her cottage was on the edge of town, away from everyone. Too bad the buggy needed to be returned for the night.

Howie saw her inside and made sure she was comfortable before returning the buggy. She lit the fire while he was gone and put the kettle on to boil while she waited for him. It seemed like an eternity before he was back, and she rushed out to the front door where he was removing his snow-covered coat. "It's cold out there," he muttered, his eyes watching her every move.

"I've lit the fire. Come over and warm up," she said, rubbing her hands together. Just having the front door open had brought in some of the chilly night air.

"I have a better way to warm up," he said quietly. When she nodded her agreement, he scooped her up and headed for the bedroom. Their bedroom from now on.

Most of Howie's belongings were still in the spare room, and Noelle decided to finish moving them into their bedroom while he was out. It had been over a week since his first night in her bed, and she wanted him to feel completely at home. As she lifted his travel bag, a piece of paper fluttered to the floor. She bent to pick it up, and her heart thudded.

Tears filled her eyes as she looked it over.

She heard the front door open, and Howie strolled in with not a care in the world. How could that be when her world had just been turned upside down? She brushed at her cheeks, trying to conceal her tears before Howie found her.

"There you are. What are you up to?" His gaze suddenly turned to the item in her hand. "I'd forgotten all about that," he said, trying to make light of it.

The stagecoach ticket she held had her stomach churning. He'd planned to leave, but the accident had caused him to stay. Forced him to stay. "I'm sorry you didn't want to be here," she said quietly, trying to force back tears. She'd thought he was happy with her. But that was before their enforced marriage.

He came close to her and wrapped her in his arms. "I didn't want to leave, not really. The trouble was, I had fallen in love with you. I knew you didn't reciprocate and thought it best to leave." He pulled her closer and kissed her forehead.

"I have been in love with you almost from the day we met."

"Almost? What did I do to deserve that?" He chuckled at his own words.

"You forced your way into my book club under false pretenses, that's what." Noelle glanced up at her husband and licked her lips. Before she could say another word, he leaned down and kissed her. Soon, he lifted her up and carried her to their bedroom.

Noelle was very much in love with her husband, and even forgave the townsfolk for pressuring them to marry.

All the stores on Dewberry Lane closed while the Christmas tree was erected. Music played in the background, and she leaned into her husband. His hands came up around her, and she didn't protest, not even a little. She watched as other couples did something similar and it warmed her heart.

"There you are," Mrs. Grayson said. "Isn't it beautiful? What a lovely tree to grace our wonderful Dewberry Lane."

Noelle also loved this new tradition they'd taken up. Not only the tree but having a donation box for the less fortunate, especially the children. She donated children's books as well as books for adults. Age did not lessen the pain of missing out at Christmas. Howie had taken it upon himself to donate dozens of stuffed toys, which would all go to good use. He was a big softie, and she knew it.

Soon, they would spend their first Christmas together, and excitement ran through her. They wouldn't have a big celebration, but she'd already began to prepare for the day by baking a Christmas cake, her first ever. Howie had ordered some other Christmas goodies from the *Holly-Berry Cake Shoppe*, so they certainly wouldn't go hungry. He'd also bought candies from *Candies Galore*, which was also on Dewberry Lane. She had some lovely glass bowls that had been her grandmother's and would use those for the candies.

In short, Howie was spoiling her. He said he wouldn't have it any other way.

Epilogue

One year later…

"This is our last book club of the year," Noelle said before the meeting began. All the ladies clutched their copy of *Hannah's Ambition*. It had been his best book to date his publisher had told him, and Howie thought the same himself. First copies had been shipped to Dewberry; express delivery at their customer's request.

His favorite place to write was still in the *Book Time* bookstore, where his wife was close by, and he spent most days there. It had become a tradition that on book club evening, they went out for supper, always at *Ma's Kitchen,* where it was homely and welcoming.

Howie often thought back to when he'd arrived in Dewberry, and the people he'd met. He still had a chuckle about the reception he'd received from his wife, not to mention Mrs. Grayson, who'd seen right through him.

"Well, Mr. Jones," Mrs. Grayson said matter-of-factly, "I do agree with the reviews. This was an interesting story. I wonder where you got the idea for the small town with its lovely little shopping strip?"

Everyone laughed and he felt heat crawl up his face.

A passionate discussion began, and everyone gave their opinion. Most of the ladies loved it, but a few were affronted, believing themselves to be portrayed in the story. Howie assured them it wasn't true. Soon they broke up for supper.

"Let me take the baby," Mrs. Grayson said, her arms outstretched. After all, Howie couldn't carry a tray of coffees and a baby at the same time.

Jacob Charles was almost three months old and was perfectly behaved. He loved being coddled by the older ladies, and not once complained at being handed around. "I'll get the Christmas cake," Noelle said, and the pair hurried into the tiny kitchen. When they were alone, Howie pulled her close and hugged Noelle tight.

"Do you know how much I love you?" he asked right before rubbing his hands over her bulging belly. "These two will be so close in age they'll be the best of friends." He leaned in and kissed her before pouring the coffees then snatched up the tray of the steaming mugs.

"I love you too," Noelle said, reaching for his hand as she felt the first flutter of their new baby.

Howie loved his wife more than life itself, and thanked the Lord for bringing him to Dewberry and blessing him with a family to love.

When he stepped off that stagecoach, he had no idea what life had in store for him, but he was so glad his life had changed for the better when he met Noelle.

The End

From the Author

Thank you so much for reading my book – I hope you enjoyed it.

I would greatly appreciate you leaving a review where you purchased, even if it is only a one-liner. It helps to have my books more visible!

About the

Author

Multi-published, award-winning and bestselling author, Cheryl Wright, former secretary, debt collector, account manager, writing coach, and shopping tour hostess, loves reading.

She writes both historical and contemporary western romance, as well as romantic suspense.

She lives in Melbourne, Australia, and is married with two adult children and has six grandchildren. When she's not writing, she can be found in her craft room making greeting cards.

Links:

Website: *http://www.cheryl-wright.com/*

Blog: *http://romance-authors.com/*

Facebook Reader Group:
https://www.facebook.com/groups/cherylwrightauthor/

Join My Newsletter:

https://cheryl-wright.com/newsletter/

WINTER'S MOTHER 1

To request permission, contact the author:
laelia@starlaarts.com

Cover illustration © Jana Hoffmann
Graphics & book design by L. Starla
Editing by Felix Staica

First edition 2021.

ISBN-13 (Paperback) 978-0-6452783-5-4
ISBN-13 (eBook) 978-0-6452783-4-7

Winter's Mother 1

Winter's Magic Part 3

L. STARLA